Cool Dog, School Dog

Story by
Deborah Heiligman

illustrated by
Tim Bowers

SCHOLASTIC INC.
New York Toronto London Auckland
Sydney Mexico City New Delhi Hong Kong

ISBN 978-0-545-28092-1

Text copyright © 2009 by Deborah Heiligman.
Illustrations copyright © 2009 by Tim Bowers. All rights reserved.
Published by Scholastic Inc., 557 Broadway, New York, NY 10012,
by arrangement with Marshall Cavendish Corporation. SCHOLASTIC and
associated logos are trademarks and/or registered trademarks of Scholastic Inc.

12 11 10 9 8 7 6 5 4 3 2   10 11 12 13 14 15/0

Printed in the U.S.A.   08

This edition first printing, September 2010

The illustrations are rendered in acrylic paint on three-ply bristol board.
Editor: Margery Cuyler
Book design by Anahid Hamparian

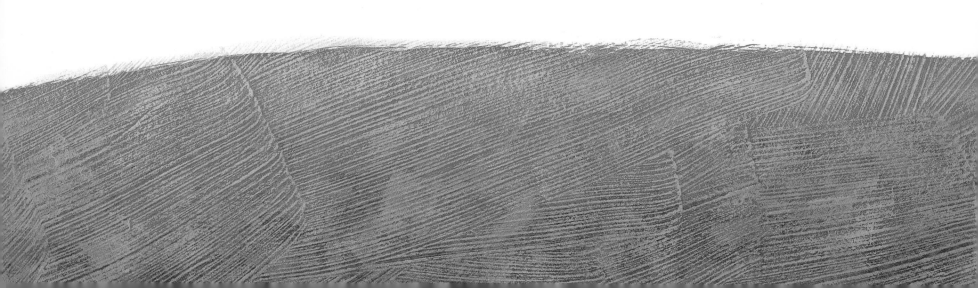

For Julia, Natalie, Amy, and Rick Sams, who were there at the beginning —D.H.

To my good friend, Joe Hickman —T.B.

Tinka is a fun dog,
a sun dog,
a run-and-run-and-run dog.

A joy dog,
a boy's dog,
a chews-a-brand-new-toy dog.

A sigh dog,
a cry dog,
a has-to-say-good-bye dog.

Tinka is a groan dog,
a moan dog,
a hates-to-be-alone dog.

A peek dog,

a sneak dog,

a spring-and-sprint-and-streak dog.

Tinka is a cool dog,
a school dog,

a breaking-all-the-rules dog.

A hall dog,
a ball dog,

a crash-into-the-wall dog.

A vroom dog,
a boom dog,
a messing-up-the-room dog.

Tinka is a bad dog,
a sad dog,
a makes-our-teacher-mad dog!

A "hey!" dog,
a "stay" dog,
a has-to-go-away dog.

A plead dog,
a need dog,
a come-help-us-to-read dog.

Tinka is a sweet dog,
a treat dog,
a-sitting-in-her-seat dog.

A look dog,
a nook dog,
a loves-to-hear-a-book dog.

a please-come-every-day dog!